Dive
Right In

by Alison Hart
illustrated by Arcana Studios

★ AmericanGirl®

Questions or comments? Call 1-800-845-0005, visit americangirl.com,
or write to Customer Service, American Girl, 8400 Fairway Place,
Middleton, WI 53562-0497.

Printed in China
11 12 13 14 15 16 LEO 10 9 8 7 6 5 4 3 2 1

All American Girl and Innerstar University marks and Amber™, Emmy™,
Isabel™, Logan™, Neely™, Paige™, Riley™, and Shelby™ are trademarks
of American Girl, LLC.

Illustrations by Thu Thai at Arcana Studios

Special thanks to Whitney Michael, USA Diving Safety–certified coach,
University of Wisconsin Diving Clinics

Cataloging-in-Publication Data available from the Library of Congress.

INNERSTARU.COM

Welcome to Innerstar University! At this imaginary, one-of-a-kind school, you can live with your friends in a dorm called Brightstar House and find lots of fun ways to let your true talents shine. Your friends at Innerstar U will help you find your way through some challenging situations, too.

When you reach a page in this book that asks you to make a decision, choose carefully. The decisions you make will lead to more than 20 different endings! (*Hint:* Use a pencil to check off your choices. That way, you'll never read the same story twice.)

Want to try another ending? Read the book again—and then again. Find out what would have happened if you'd made *different* choices. Then head to www.innerstarU.com for even more book endings, games, and fun with friends.

Innerstar Guides

Every girl needs a few good friends to help her find her way. These are the friends who are always there for **you**.

Emmy

A brave girl who loves swimming and boating

Isabel

A confident girl with a funky sense of style

Riley

A good sport, on the field and off

Paige

A nature lover who leads hikes and campus cleanups

Amber

An animal lover and
a loyal friend

Neely

A creative girl who loves
dance, music, and art

Logan

A super-smart girl
who is curious about
EVERYTHING

Shelby

A kind girl who is there
for her friends—and loves
making NEW friends!

Innerstar U Campus

1. Rising Star Stables
2. Star Student Center
3. Brightstar House
4. Starlight Library
5. Sparkle Studios
6. Blue Sky Nature Center

7. Real Spirit Center
8. Five-Points Plaza
9. Starfire Lake & Boathouse
10. U-Shine Hall
11. Good Sports Center
12. Shopping Square
13. The Market
14. Morningstar Meadow

[R] iley, Emmy!" you call from the three-meter springboard to two of your diving teammates. You're at the Good Sports Center, ready to dive into the clear pool. "Any advice on how to improve my back dive?" you ask. You want to nail the "back dive straight" for the upcoming interscholastic competition.

"Use your eyes," Emmy suggests. "But don't look back until after you've 'set' your arms." Emmy is the number-one diver on the team, just ahead of you.

"Arch backward a little more when you take off," Riley adds. Riley may not be number one on the team, but she's number one at helping her teammates.

You nod and walk to the end of the board. Turning around, you stretch your arms high and balance on the balls of your feet. You spring up, set your arms in a T position, arch slightly, and then start looking for the water. As you drop, your arms come together over your head. You line up tight and slice into the cool water.

When your head pops to the surface, you're grinning. There's no better feeling than doing a great dive!

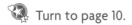 Turn to page 10.

"Yay!" Riley cheers.

"A perfect 10!" says Emmy, holding up ten fingers.

As you climb up the ladder, you spot Jamie, another teammate, walking into the pool area with your good friend Megan behind her. You're surprised to see Megan here. She's a gymnast, not a diver.

"Megan!" you exclaim, giving her a wet hug. "What are you doing here?"

"*Eww*, you're soaked," Megan says, grinning as she pulls away and shakes the water off her arms. "I'm here to join the team. You're always talking about how fun it is."

"It *is* fun," says Jamie, "and we can definitely use more members."

"You'll be a great addition to the team," Riley adds.

Emmy nods. "And your gymnastics training will be a huge help in learning the dives," she says.

You smile at Megan. "It's official, then," you say. "Welcome to the Innerstar U diving team!"

 Turn to page 12.

Coach comes up and welcomes Megan, too. Then she suggests that you and Emmy take Megan into the practice room for some dryland work. Practice on floor mats and the trampoline is an important part of training.

Using a dryland springboard and a cushioned landing pit, you demonstrate the approach and the hurdle. Then you and Emmy explain the different positions. "During the *flight* of the dive, which is when you are in the air, there are three positions," you tell Megan.

Emmy points to the first of three posters on the wall. "In the straight position, you can't bend in the knees or hips," she explains.

"In a pike position, you keep your knees straight but bend forward and reach for your toes," you continue.

"In the tuck, you curl your body into a ball," Emmy says, tapping the third poster. "You hold your shins and point your toes."

"Wow," Megan gasps, her eyes wide. "This is awesome. I can't wait to get on a real diving board!"

Megan soon gets her wish. In the next few weeks, you and your teammates help her with the front, back, and inward dives from the one-meter and three-meter springboards. Megan is a natural, and her gymnastics training definitely helps.

You're excited for your friend and proud of her ability. But every once in a while, you feel a twinge of jealousy. You've worked hard all *year*, and it doesn't seem fair that Megan catches on so easily.

One day, Coach spends the whole practice working on *lineups*, or how to position your body when you enter the water. Megan fidgets, as if she's getting bored. Finally she leans over and whispers, "When do we get to do twists and somersaults? I'm ready to do the exciting stuff."

"Soon," you whisper back. "But this is important for the competition. The judges take off points for the takeoff, flight, and entry. We have to do each of them right."

"Oh. Gotcha," Megan says. You hope she does. It's true that the trickier dives are way more fun. But the basics are important, too, if the diving team is going to win.

 Turn to page 14.

The next day you ask Coach if you can practice some harder dives. Your teammates cheer at your suggestion.

"We should do the front somersault full twist," says Jamie.

Your brows shoot up. That *is* trickier! You've spent the last week working on it.

Coach asks you to demonstrate while she explains each step. You smile confidently as you climb up onto the one-meter board. You start your approach, spring from the board, and perform a somersault in the open pike position. You snap to a layout—twisting in the air with your legs together. Then you square out, unwinding your arms to stop the twist. You enter the water smoothly.

"Woo-hoo!" your teammates holler as you swim to the ladder.

"Looks like fun! I'm ready to try it," Megan says. "Somersaults and twists are my favorite in gymnastics." Eagerly she climbs onto the board. You watch her dive as you dry off with your chamois. As Megan twists through the air, your jaw drops. Her first try is almost as good as yours!

 If you squelch your jealousy and compliment Megan, turn to page 16.

 If you decide to do a dive that you know Megan can't do, turn to page 17.

"Great dive, Megan," you say, praising her.

Megan climbs from the pool. She's all smiles as the team crowds around her. "Thanks, guys," she says. "That dive is a lot like a dismount I do on the balance beam. That's why it wasn't too hard for me."

Hearing that makes you feel better. And, after all, you *should* want Megan to do well. Her talent will help the team win the upcoming competition. Diving is an individual sport, so each diver is rated by five judges and given a total score. But Innerstar U competes as a team, too. You want your team to win, so you plunge into helping Megan master more dives.

"Let's try the same dive but with a one-and-a-half somersault and a twist," you suggest.

Megan eagerly nods. All the girls try it, and once again, Megan manages to pull off the dive.

"Wow, Megan," Jamie says as she dries off. "Pretty soon you'll be better than your friend here." Jamie nods in your direction.

Everyone looks at you. You can feel your face flush with embarrassment. Is Jamie right?

 If you swallow your pride and agree with Jamie, turn to page 18.

 If you disagree with Jamie, turn to page 20.

"I'm going to do a double twisting one-and-a-half," you announce as you march to the three-meter board.

Riley lets out a tiny gasp. That's the toughest dive you've worked on so far—on dryland. You haven't tried it on the springboard yet.

"That sounds cool!" Megan exclaims.

All eyes turn to you as you climb the ladder. You gulp. On dryland, you had that second twist down. You take a deep breath, hoping you can nail it from the board, too.

You throw for the somersault and wrap high for the two twists, but you square out a bit early before plunging into the pool.

Still, cheers greet you as you swim to the surface.

"I've gotta try that!" Megan exclaims.

"Haven't you practiced somersaults only on the trampoline?" Riley asks.

"Yeah, but I did them all the time in gymnastics," says Megan. Without hesitating, she hurries onto the board and does a pretty good imitation of your dive.

"Wow," Emmy says when Megan pops to the surface. "With a little practice, you're going to be the best diver on this team."

You stare at Emmy, who is smiling and seems more impressed by Megan than jealous. So why does Megan's talent bother *you* so much?

 Turn to page 21.

"That's great if Megan is better than I am," you say, trying to sound super happy. "We want the team to win the next competition, right?"

"Right!" the other girls chorus. As you head to the locker room, everyone is chattering excitedly. You're glad that you kept your hurt pride to yourself.

The next day the team works on the trampoline. First you practice somersaults, and Megan demonstrates some techniques she learned in gymnastics. Then Coach comes in to help you practice trickier moves.

"You first, Megan," Coach says. "We'll put you in the belts." She straps Megan into a harness. The harness hooks to a pulley over the trampoline so that Megan can bounce high in the air and practice twists and dives safely.

This is the first time Megan has been strapped in the belts, but she leaps and twists as if she's been doing it her whole life.

"Way to go, Megan!" Emmy exclaims.

"This is incredible," Megan gasps. "It's like flying!"

As Megan rotates in the air, most of the girls cheer her on. You notice that Jamie, who always has something to say, is oddly silent. And you aren't cheering as loudly for your friend as you should be.

What's wrong with me? you wonder. You're proud that your friend is doing so well, and you do want her on the team. But could she not be *quite* so wonderful?

 Turn to page 22.

Jamie is *not* right, you decide grumpily. Megan just started diving. You've been practicing all season. Sure, Megan has natural talent. But there is no way you're going to let her become a better diver than you.

The next day you come to practice early. You ask Coach to spot you on the trampoline. You want to perfect those kickouts and twists.

You're in the middle of a twist when Emmy and Riley come into the exercise room. When you jump off the trampoline, Emmy asks, "What's going on? Does Coach want you to do extra training?"

"No, I decided I needed extra practice," you explain. "I'm worried about the competition."

Emmy and Riley exchange looks, as if they know that's not the only reason. Do they guess it's also because you're determined not to let Megan best you?

 Turn to page 23.

The next day you get to the sports center early. You decide that it's time you showed up Megan by doing something she *isn't* great at. You don't remember her ever practicing back flips on the trampoline.

Coach spots you in the harness until you've polished up your back one-and-a-half. When the girls arrive for practice, you make sure that Megan sees you do it off the springboard into the pool.

"That's awesome!" she exclaims. "I've gotta try it. Can you give me some pointers?"

"Umm, it's pretty tricky, Megan," you warn.

"Backs can't be that much harder than fronts," she says, climbing onto the springboard. You're sure she'll blow the dive, but at least that will prove to her that she needs to quit being such a daredevil.

Megan tackles the dive, kicking out early. Her heel hits the end of the board with a loud *thunk*, making you wince. When her head surfaces, you kneel on the edge of the pool.

"Are you all right?" you ask. You didn't want Megan to hurt herself. You just wanted her to realize that diving takes practice, patience, and hard work.

 Turn to page 24.

In the locker room after practice, Megan admires your new duffel bag. "Where'd you get that?" she asks.

"Girl Gear," you reply. "I'll bet there are still some left. Should we go look?" Maybe a shopping trip will head off that jealousy you've been feeling.

"Great idea," Megan says. As the two of you walk, all Megan talks about is diving. "I'm so psyched about the competition," she gushes. "I really, really want to work on some of the hard, optional dives. I need those points if I'm going to win."

Megan is talking so fast, your head is spinning. "Slow down, Megan," you finally say. "Winning isn't everything."

"Oh, but it is!" she exclaims.

She's joking, right? You can't tell. You never realized how much Megan loves to win. You hope her competitive spirit doesn't get in the way of your friendship.

If you decide to talk to Megan about your worries, turn to page 25.

If you don't say anything, turn to page 28.

For the rest of the week and all weekend, you come in early and stay late to practice. The extra time pays off—your form is cleaner and sharper. But by Sunday night, you're exhausted. You stagger back to your dorm room at Brightstar House and find your friend Shelby waiting for you in the hall.

"Ready to work on our history project?" she asks eagerly.

You stare at Shelby, trying to figure out what she's talking about. She's carrying a poster board and markers. *Oh no.* You totally forgot you had to find facts and photos on Greek architecture!

Your shoulders slump. "I'm sorry, Shelby," you say. "I've been spending so much time at the pool that I forgot."

"Eek!" Shelby squeals. "How could you forget? The project is due Tuesday. I need an A to pass the course!"

"I'm *sorry*," you say again, only this time it sounds as if you're snapping at her. Maybe you are. Right now, you're so tired, you can't even think about homework. "We'll get it done tomorrow," you reassure her.

But Shelby doesn't seem convinced. "Don't worry about it. I'll do it myself," she says as she turns and walks away.

You watch her until she disappears around a corner. You should go after her and apologize, but you're just too tired.

 Turn to page 26.

Megan nods. "I just whacked my foot," she says. She limps into the locker room and sits on the bench. You and your diving coach follow her in, and the two of you bustle around, getting Megan an ice pack and a towel.

"Really, I'm okay," Megan says again. She twists her foot in the air. "See? No damage."

You give Megan a genuine smile of concern as you sit next to her. What were you thinking? You should have told her how much you practiced on dryland before attempting the back one-and-a-half in the water.

"Keep the ice on your heel," Coach suggests. "There's going to be a bruise."

"Bruises are nothing," Megan says. "We fell all the time in gymnastics. But maybe I'll sit out practice tomorrow . . . just in case."

The worry in Megan's voice makes you want to kick yourself. Megan is your teammate and one of your best friends. Yet your hurt pride turned you against her. You need to figure out a way to make it up to her.

 If you decide to be a better friend and teammate, turn to page 27.

If you decide to confess to Megan how you've been feeling, turn to page 29.

You wait until the next day to talk to Megan. You catch up with her in the locker room before practice.

"Hey, Megan," you begin. "There's something that's kind of worrying me."

Megan closes her locker and sits on the bench beside you. "What is it?" she asks. She looks so concerned that you almost lose your nerve.

You take a deep breath. "Well, I'm worried that our friendship is going to be all about diving," you confess. "I don't want to miss the fun times we had together *before* dive team."

Megan looks surprised. "But we'll have even more fun now that I'm on the team," she says. "I love diving! In fact, I've decided to quit gymnastics and focus on diving. Coach told me that with hard work, I might qualify for nationals someday."

Nationals! You're stunned. Only the top six divers from each region qualify for nationals. Jamie and Riley, who have just come into the locker room, overhear Megan's comment, too.

Jamie snorts. "That's a crazy dream," she says. "Only divers who have worked for *years* make nationals."

"Oh, I don't know," Riley says. "I think Megan should go for her dream."

 If you agree with Jamie, turn to page 31.

 If you agree with Riley, turn to page 41.

Monday morning, you run into Megan coming down the hall. She's carrying her duffel bag.

"Where are you going so early?" you ask.

"To practice the front two-and-a-half before class," she says. Her eyes are bright with excitement.

The two-and-a-half! You've practiced that dive on dry-land but never off the boards. You can't let Megan learn it before you do.

That afternoon, you practice the two-and-a-half on the trampoline. Emmy helps out, giving you pointers as you somersault in the belts.

"Let's try it on the diving board," you tell her. You're breathless after all those spins, but you're eager to keep going.

"Sorry—I'm going kayaking with Riley this afternoon," Emmy says. "I'll help you tomorrow."

But tomorrow will be too late if you're going to perform the dive before Megan. You decide to head to the pool by yourself. Coach is there and can give you pointers.

When you're standing on the springboard, though, your confidence takes a nosedive. If you don't make that second somersault, you could hit the water awkwardly. Your head hurts at the thought of it.

 If you go for the dive anyway, turn to page 30.

 If you chicken out, turn to page 42.

The next day, instead of getting to the pool early so that you can practice by yourself, you rally the team for a game of "who can do the silliest dive."

"We've been working so hard," you explain to your teammates. "We deserve some fun."

"I agree," Jamie says as she follows you toward the board. You notice Megan is hanging back. At least she isn't limping today. You hope your silly dives will draw her into the game.

Running down the board, you spring into the air, grab your shins, and cannonball into the water. When you come up out of the water, you see Riley laughing by the side of the pool. She's soaking wet.

"That splash was eight feet high!" she announces, wiping the water out of her eyes.

"That's nothing," Jamie says just before she, too, cannonballs into the pool.

Soon everyone is trying to beat one another's "splash"— everyone but Megan, who sits on the pool edge.

"Megan!" you call. "Your turn."

Megan hesitates for a moment but then smiles and heads for the board. Instead of a cannonball, she does a crazy leap, arms and feet wiggling in the air. That starts a whole new round of silly dives. You're cracking up at your teammates' creativity.

 Turn to page 32.

You think back to when you first joined the team. You were totally focused on the sport and nervous about doing well. Maybe Megan is feeling nervous, too. You decide to help her by being a more supportive friend.

"Are you still doing gymnastics?" you ask, hoping to get Megan's mind on something besides diving.

She shrugs. "I still go once a week," she says. "But gymnastics is a club. We don't compete. That's one reason I joined diving—because I love competing." She thinks for a moment and then asks, "Tell me again how the judges score during the competition?"

Here we go again, you think. *Right back to diving*. You take a deep breath and explain the scoring system: "There are five judges who score each dive. The highest and lowest scores are crossed out. The other three are added together, and that total is multiplied by the 'degree of difficulty' for the dive. A good score is a six or seven. A ten, the highest score, is pretty impossible."

Megan lets out a huge sigh. "Gymnastics club was easy compared to diving," she says. "There's so much to learn that sometimes I feel as if my head is going to explode."

You stare at your friend. You had no idea she was so stressed. What can you do to help her have more fun?

If you suggest going with her to gymnastics, turn to page 38.

If you suggest inline skating, turn to page 44.

Swallowing your pride, you make a confession to Megan. "I had to practice the back one-and-a-half for a long time on dryland before I could do it off the board," you say. "I shouldn't have let you try it without practicing on the trampoline first."

"It's okay," Megan says, shrugging.

But it's not okay with you. Your jealousy got in the way of your friendship, and you need to make it up to Megan. "Next time, I'll help you with your dives instead of trying to show off my own skills," you promise her. "Even better, we'll work on new dives together."

"There probably won't be a next time," Megan says.

You stare at her. "What do you mean?" you ask.

Taking her foot off the ice pack, she studies her heel. There's already a purple bruise forming where she hit it. Finally, she says, "I've decided that diving is not for me. I'm quitting and going back to gymnastics."

You're stunned. Megan is a natural at diving. Did your behavior make her dislike diving? Or was it her botched dive? Either way, it's your fault!

 Turn to page 36.

Just then Megan comes into the pool area. She sees you poised on the board. You have to conquer that front two-and-a-half if you want to hang on to any shred of pride.

You fake confidence and launch into the dive, thinking about how surprised your friend will be when she sees you do it. But spinning on the trampoline in belts is easier than spinning from a diving board. Your hurdle is off, and after the last rotation, you kick out early, smacking your legs on the water. *Ouch!*

As you climb from the water, Megan hurries over, her eyes wide with surprise. Is she surprised that you tried the two-and-a-half? Surprised that you did it before she could? Or surprised that you blew it?

Before Megan can say anything, Coach comes over. Checking your reddening skin, she says, "Maybe you should take a break."

You nod and trudge toward the locker room, your confidence shaken. Megan is watching you, but that's okay. You left your pride behind somewhere in the deep end of that pool.

 Turn to page 33.

"Megan, I know you love diving," you tell your friend. "But you just started. What makes you think you can get to nationals?"

Jamie steps up beside you, a disgusted look on her face. "Yeah, Megan, get real," she says. "You may be good, but you're no C. J. Wirkus."

With that, Jamie walks off to start warming up.

"C. J. who?" Megan asks.

"C. J. Wirkus. She's only the best diver who ever went to Innerstar U," Riley gushes. "Her name is all over the plaques in our trophy case."

Megan's face reddens with embarrassment and the sting of Jamie's words.

Sighing, you realize that your question must have sounded harsh, too, as if you didn't believe in your friend. But, really—nationals? So soon?

 Turn to page 34.

When practice begins, you are happy to see that Megan is joining in rather than sitting out. Your silly dives did the trick! And when Coach announces it's time to work on dives, Megan says that she wants to master the back one-and-a-half. That's the dive she was doing yesterday when she hit her heel.

Coach takes Megan and Emmy to the trampoline while you, Riley, and Jamie practice some required dives. When Megan comes back, she's beaming. This time, she does a pretty decent back one-and-a-half, kicking out perfectly.

When Jamie says to you, "Wow, that dive was better than yours," you smile and agree. You're proud of your friend, and you're a teeny bit proud of yourself, too. You chose to be a good role model, helping Megan gain back her confidence.

That pride gives *you* confidence as you head to the springboard, ready to tackle another tricky dive.

The End

"Wait up!" Megan calls, jogging after you. You tense up, waiting for her to tell you how lousy your dive was. But she surprises you by saying, "Great try! I had a hard time with the two-and-a-half when I tried it this morning."

"Thanks," you mumble. Then you launch into the list of mistakes you made, beginning with the hurdle.

"Some of that might be true," Megan says, "but my gymnastics coach always told me to focus on what I did *right*."

You stare at her. How can Megan be so nice to you when you've been so, well, *not* nice lately?

"You did a lot of things right," Megan goes on. "Maybe tomorrow, we can practice takeoffs on the trampoline together. I bet we can both hit those two-and-a-halfs."

You hesitate. Part of you just doesn't want to practice with Megan. Maybe it's because once again, she's better than you—better at being a good friend.

If you need a break from diving and Megan, turn to page 68.

If you accept Megan's offer to practice together, turn to page 37.

During practice, you try to cheer Megan on. You wish you could go back to that first day when you were *glad* that Megan was joining the team.

Sighing, you head to the locker room before the others to shower and change. When you step from the shower stall, you see Jamie holding Megan's new duffel bag. She has a goofy grin on her face.

"Shhh," Jamie whispers, putting a finger to her lips. "I'm hiding her bag. She needs to get knocked off her 'high dive' a little."

You open your mouth to stop Jamie, but then you say nothing. Jamie loves pranks and has played plenty of them on you. A part of you is glad that this time, the prank's on someone else.

Megan comes into the locker room with Emmy and Riley. The three are chatting and laughing. Megan's laughter stops abruptly when she can't find her new bag. "Hey, have you seen my bag?" she asks you.

"Umm . . ." you look at Jamie, who starts to giggle.

Megan puts her fists on her hips. "What's going on?" she asks. "I need my towel and clothes."

"I didn't take it," Jamie says, sounding totally innocent.

Megan's eyes stare accusingly at you.

"I'm sure it's here somewhere," says Riley. She and Emmy start searching spare lockers and finally come across the bag. Emmy pulls it out and hands it to Megan.

 Turn to page 40.

POOL THIS WAY

"Megan, you can't quit," you protest. "You're one of the best divers on the team. That's why I get so jealous sometimes."

Now it's her turn to look surprised. "You were jealous of me?" she asks. "I was jealous of you! You always made everything look so easy."

"I just never wanted to let on about how much I had to practice," you admit.

When you realize that you were both feeling the same way, you and Megan laugh together—just the way you used to.

"So, will you stay on the team?" you ask.

Megan shakes her head. "Nope," she says. "I've decided that my heart is in gymnastics."

Megan sounds sure of her decision, so you need to accept it. It *does* mean no more competing with her. That's what you wanted, right?

Wrong. Megan quitting doesn't really make you happy. You wish you could have supported her when she was having problems. You were so focused on being the best diver. You should have focused, instead, on being a better *friend*.

The End

You agree to practice with Megan. She's being extra nice, and practicing together might help repair your strained friendship.

On the trampoline with Coach spotting, Megan takes only a few tries to get the rotations down. But when you try the moves, fear still makes your insides spin.

"I don't know what's wrong," you say. Actually, you *do* know, but Megan is such a daredevil that you don't think she would understand the words "I'm scared."

"Try again," Megan suggests. "You'll get it."

You're already unbuckling your harness. "I'll try again tomorrow," you say. "I have a history test that I need to study for, so I need to cut practice short."

"Hey, I have the same history test," Megan says. "Do you want to study together?"

"Great idea!" you say. You try to sound upbeat, but you feel anything but that inside. You can't understand why the two-and-a-half is so difficult for you—especially when Megan makes it look easy. Has your pride sunk so low that fear has taken its place?

 Turn to page 47.

"You sound stressed out," you tell Megan. "Let's plan something fun. I've always wanted to try gymnastics. Can I join you the next time you go?"

Megan's eyes brighten. "Sure!" she says. "How about tomorrow? We can practice somersaults. I need to make them tighter for diving." *Ugh*—there's that word again. Okay, you didn't totally get Megan's mind off diving, but it's a start.

The next day, you meet Megan at the sports center. It feels weird to be wearing your shorts and T-shirt instead of your swimsuit. Megan's wearing a leotard.

The instructor breaks you into groups. You're with the beginners, of course, but quickly get switched to a higher group. You recognize a friend in the group—Isabel. She's wearing a paisley leotard, stylish as always.

"Try the balance beam," Isabel encourages you. You watch her use the springboard to mount the balance beam. It's sort of like a tiny diving board, so you think this should be easy.

Not. You spring too high, flying over the beam and landing on the mats on the other side. You are laughing so hard, you can barely stand up. Isabel and the others in your group burst out laughing with you. Maybe you needed this time to relax just as much as Megan did.

 Turn to page 55.

After changing her clothes, Megan hurries off with Emmy and Riley. She won't even look at you. Alone, you head to the cafeteria and make your way to the salad bar.

When you sit down to eat, Jamie joins you. She's smiling secretively. "I've got an even better prank to play on Megan tomorrow," she whispers as she slides into the seat next to yours. "I'm going to put lemon juice in her water bottle. Can you imagine the look on her face when she takes a big swig?" Jamie bursts out laughing.

"Jamie, don't you think you're going too far?" you ask.

"No. I'm tired of Megan thinking she's better than the rest of us," says Jamie. She's obviously mad that you don't agree with her.

You finish your salad in silence. You understand why Jamie's mad. Since Megan joined the team, everything has changed. But that doesn't mean you should act like Jamie, you decide. You need to apologize to Megan right away.

Standing up, you clear your tray. You need to find your friend and apologize for questioning her dream. Sure, your pride is bruised, but you're going to move past it. Megan might become number one, beating you, but that doesn't mean you can't be Megan's number-one fan—and friend.

The End

"A goal is good motivation," you say.

Megan nods enthusiastically. "I'm reading online about national champions who started training in their sports at our age."

"Really?" you say. "That's cool!"

Jamie frowns. "You guys are crazy," she scoffs. "The only thing I dream about is scoring sevens in the upcoming competition."

You do think Megan's dreams are pretty out of this world, but you admire her determination. Megan's goals and enthusiasm might be just what you—and the team— need right now.

If you ask Megan to show you the online site, turn to page 43.

If you ask Megan if you can train with her, turn to page 50.

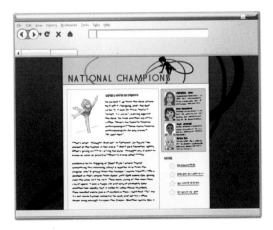

Pulse racing, you walk to the end of the board. You bounce a few times, trying to picture yourself doing the two-and-a-half. You wince as you imagine yourself coming out of the last rotation and hitting the water hard.

Admit it, you think. *You're so chicken that feathers could sprout from your arms at any moment.* You just aren't ready.

You bounce high and do a reverse dive pike instead, as if that's what you meant to do all along. After you kick to the surface, you paddle slowly to the ladder. Why did you want to rush learning a new dive, anyway? Then you spot Megan coming in to practice. She's giggling with Jamie as they head for the diving boards.

Megan is the reason. Since she joined the team, everything has changed. Your pride in your dives went out the door, and now you're frantically trying to get it back by pushing yourself.

As you climb from the pool, you watch Megan perform the two-and-a-half without hesitation. Her confidence and talent shine like stars.

Your heart sinks.

 Turn to page 46.

That night after dinner, you poke your head into Megan's room. She's slouched in her desk chair, studying.

"Reading about champions?" you ask her.

Megan looks up from her book and grins. "I wish!" she says. "But no. I'm reading our history homework."

"Do you have a sec to show me that website?" you ask.

"Sure!" says Megan. She swivels her chair toward her computer. "I have it bookmarked along with a website on nationals," she explains, pulling up both sites.

Megan really *is* serious. You jot down the web address. Later, back in your room, you look up the site and read story after story about committed athletes. Most devote all their time to training. Some even move to be near the best coaches. Wow. You had no idea. The amount of energy these athletes put into their sports makes you feel tired.

"Knock, knock," someone says, startling you. It's your friend Amber. "Am I interrupting?" she asks.

"No. I was just reading about diving champions," you say, sounding as depressed as you suddenly feel. "There's no way I want to spend every free hour diving. Maybe I should give it up."

"But you *love* diving like I love riding," Amber says. "It sounds as if you just need a break. Why not take a day off tomorrow and join me at the stables?"

You like Amber's idea. Maybe a day off will bring back that enthusiasm.

 Turn to page 52.

"Megan, you sound stressed out," you say gently. "Let's do something fun that has *nothing* to do with diving."

"Like what?" she asks.

"How about skating?" you ask. "Remember when we rented inline skates and hit the path by the park?"

"But we were *terrible*," Megan groans.

"That's the point!" you say. "We were so terrible that we spent most of the time laughing."

Megan tilts her head and smiles. "I guess I could use a little of that," she says. "Okay, let's do it."

The next day the two of you rent skates, helmets, and pads at the sports center. Holding hands, you skate down the path toward the park, the wind brushing against your cheeks. It feels great, until you zip around a corner . . . right into a fallen branch!

"Whoa!" you holler, veering toward the grass and tumbling to the ground. Megan lands in a heap next to you. Laughing, you help each other up. *This is what it's all about,* you think to yourself, *having fun and supporting each other.*

You start off down the path again, proud that you were able to remind Megan of the good times you can have together. You know that a little laughter and fun will make you better friends—and maybe better teammates, too.

The End

Sighing, you pick up your chamois from the bench and dry off.

"Hey!" Megan calls cheerfully as she climbs out of the water.

"Hi, Megan. Great two-and-a-half," you tell her, trying to keep from choking on the praise.

"Thanks. Did you try it yet off the board?" she asks. "We saw Emmy leaving the sports center. She said you were practicing the dive in belts."

"Oh, um . . ." you stammer. What are you going to tell her? That you were too chicken? "Oh, look!" you say instead. "Riley's doing an armstand dive. Awesome!" You point to Riley, who is balancing on her hands at the end of the five-meter platform, her legs in the air.

"Yeah, she said she's going to try it off the seven-meter next," Megan explains.

You gulp. It seems as if everyone around here is fear-less—everyone except you.

Megan turns her attention back to you. "So what about that two-and-a-half?" she asks again. "How's that going?"

 If you confess your fears to Megan, turn to page 48.

 If you hide your fears, turn to page 60.

You make plans to meet Megan after dinner to study, and then you head into the locker room for a long, steamy shower. Mostly you want to be alone so that you can think.

You really don't want to study with Megan, you realize. She's one of the reasons you've been feeling so down about diving. Then why did you say yes when she asked you to study with her?

It's as if everything you say and do lately has been wrong. The truth is, since your friend's been on the team, you've even thought about quitting. You could switch to a totally different sport, like swimming or maybe horseback riding with Amber.

The shower leaves you feeling squeaky clean, but you're still lost in gloomy thoughts as you get dressed and head out the door. Riley catches up with you just outside the sports center. She must notice your slumped shoulders because she says, "You seem kind of down. Is something wrong?"

If you tell Riley that you're thinking of quitting the team, turn to page 51.

If you mumble something about the upcoming history test, turn to page 58.

"Great!" you squeak, sounding like a rubber duck. But then you slump onto the bench. It's time you stopped blaming your problems with the dive on Megan. It's time you admitted that your lack of confidence kept you frozen on the diving board.

Sighing, you say, "The truth is, Megan, I was way too scared to try the dive off the board."

Tossing down her chamois, Megan stands up. "Well, then, let's work on it together," she says. "That's how I get over my fears."

"You? Fears?" you ask.

"Of course," she says. "It took Coach and Riley forever to convince me I could do the two-and-a-half on the tramp."

Your jaw drops. All this time you thought Megan had no fears. You jump up from the bench, too. When you get back up on the board, your pulse is still racing. But from down below, Megan calls encouraging words.

You take a deep breath and approach the end of the board. You hurdle into the air, spin once, twice, and then kick out and fall straight into the water. When you come up, you are grinning proudly—not because of the dive, which still needs work, but because you finally quit blaming everyone, accepted help from your friend, and took the plunge.

The End

"Training together would be fun," Megan agrees when you ask her about it. "We can help each other."

You grin excitedly. "Let's do it!" you say. The next week, you "dive" headfirst into Megan's dream of going to nationals. And why not? Part of you knows that making the national team is farfetched, but Megan's ambition has set yours on fire, too.

When Coach mentions signing up for the upcoming interscholastic competition, you and Megan pore over the list of dives. With Megan by your side, you're ready to try something new.

"What I really want to learn is an inward double on the three-meter, which I've never done before," you tell your friend. "It seems scary to me because you have to rotate *toward* the board."

Megan nods. "I know—the timing for the kickout has to be perfect," she adds. Then she looks sideways at you and grins. "Together, though, we can do it!" she says, reaching out to give you a high five.

Coach gives each of you a turn on the trampoline, and soon you and Megan are working on the inward doubles. You don't think you'd have the courage to do them without your good friend by your side.

 Turn to page 54.

As you walk together to Brightstar House, you tell Riley, "I'm really down about diving. I think I'm going to try a different sport."

"But why?" Riley asks. She sounds so concerned that you end up telling her everything.

"I'm having a terrible time learning new dives," you admit. "I never used to be afraid, but now when I try a hard move, I feel sick and want to quit."

"That's normal," Riley says. "Even Emmy feels that way sometimes when she learns a new dive, and she's number one on the team."

"Well, that's another thing," you say, because now you're on a roll. "I thought Megan joining the team would be great. Only she's so talented, she's making me green with envy. It's like I'm always in her shadow. Soon she'll take my number-two spot on the team. And I'm going to hate being bumped to number three."

Riley pats you on the shoulder. "I totally understand that feeling," she says. "Don't forget: since Megan came, I'm now number *five* on the team. And no matter how hard I try, I'll always be in your shadow."

You stop dead in your tracks. Wow, you had no idea Riley felt that way. Have you been too focused on yourself to notice?

 Turn to page 65.

The next afternoon, you slide into jeans and run to Rising Star Stables. Instead of an inside pool and diving boards, there's an outside riding ring and fences. Instead of the smell of chlorine, there's the smell of grain and hay. You breathe deeply, enjoying the change in scenery.

You find Amber just outside the stables, tacking up Silver Sky. "He's so beautiful!" you exclaim. You gently stroke Sky's side.

You watch as Amber mounts Sky. Behind her in the arena, you spot another rider. It looks like . . . Riley? You had no idea that Riley fit riding into her diving schedule.

Amber trots Sky around, a huge grin on her face. You realize that's how you should be feeling about diving. When she rides Sky over and dismounts to give you a turn, you ask, "Amber, what do you love best about riding?"

"Everything!" she says. "I love showing and competing, and I love just trotting on the trail with my friends."

You nod, but Amber's response makes you wonder what you love most about *diving*.

 If the thrill of competing tops your list, turn to page 57.

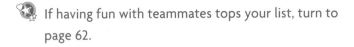 If having fun with teammates tops your list, turn to page 62.

At practice the next day, Megan has big news: "I've signed up to do a two-week diving clinic with another coach," she says. "She has a *really* good reputation."

You're shocked. Why didn't Megan mention this to you earlier? "But what about our team?" you ask her.

"Oh, I'll have time for both," Megan says. "There's another clinic starting in two weeks. Why don't you sign up, too?"

You *would* like to learn harder dives, and you've been having such fun with Megan, you don't want it to stop. "Maybe I will," you tell her.

As the days go on, you see less and less of Megan. You miss your friend and can't wait until the next clinic begins. When she brings you a clinic sign-up form before practice one day, you grab a pen and start filling it out right away.

"It starts next Saturday," Megan says as you write. "The first day is the most important because that's when they assign you to groups. I'm sure you'll be in mine."

Uh-oh. Your hand freezes. "But next Saturday is the interscholastic competition," you remind Megan.

Megan's jaw drops. "Oh, no! I forgot all about that," she says. "What are we going to do?"

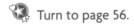 Turn to page 56.

"I had such a great time!" you tell Isabel and the others at the end of the session.

"Why don't you join the gymnastics club?" Isabel suggests. "You sure learned the exercises quickly."

You grin, thinking about how wobbly you were on the balance beam. Still, it's nice to hear some praise. "I'll definitely think about it," you tell her.

"I'm glad you had fun," Megan says as you leave the gymnasium. "I did, too."

Megan looks much more relaxed now, but as the two of you walk down the long hall of the sports center, she veers toward the pool's locker room. "Gotta practice a few dives," Megan says as she disappears through the doorway. You can't believe she's diving right after gymnastics. Your body feels like a limp noodle.

You run into your friend Neely coming from the dance studio. She's wearing warm-ups over her leotard, and her brown hair is in a bouncy ponytail. "I'll walk with you back to Brightstar House if you're going that way," she offers.

As you leave the sports center, you tell Neely how much you enjoyed gymnastics.

"Why don't you come to ballet sometime, too?" Neely asks. "There are all levels of dancers."

Why not? you think. Maybe the clue to handling your stress about Megan is trying different activities. You could use a few fun things to focus on.

 Turn to page 80.

Glancing at the form in your hand, you realize Megan is right: it's a dilemma for both of you. But then you see Riley, Jamie, and Emmy come into the locker room to get ready for practice. You feel a pang in your chest. You and Megan have gotten so carried away with your big dreams that you've kind of forgotten about your other teammates.

You crumple up the form. "Sorry, Megan," you say. "The competition next Saturday is too important. I want to support Innerstar U, and I don't want to let our teammates down. Maybe I can join the *next* clinic."

Megan sighs. "Yeah, you're right," she says. "I'll tell the clinic coach that I am already committed to the diving team, too."

You toss the crumpled form into your duffel bag. You hope that someday soon you can sign up for the clinic. For now, though, you're proud of your—and Megan's—decision to stick with your diving team. Having big dreams and goals *doesn't* mean forgetting your friends.

The End

"I love doing tricky dives," you tell Amber. "And getting high scores from the judges in competition."

Riley trots her spotted horse over to join you, Sky, and Amber. "Hi, teammate!" she says.

"Hey, Riley!" you greet her. "I didn't know you rode. How do you fit riding time into your diving schedule?"

"I'm not as competitive as you, so I don't have to practice *quite* so hard," she admits, winking at you. "I guess I'd rather make time for riding than worry about those tricky dives."

You arch one brow as you listen. *There's your answer,* you think. Maybe you're not interested in competing at nationals, but you do love the thrill of learning hard dives and competing in regional competitions.

The next day at practice, Coach announces that there'll be a mock competition in three days to prepare for the interscholastic competition.

You, not Megan, are the first to cheer. "I'm going to put a tough dive or two on my list," you tell your teammates.

"Me too. I'm going to win with a . . ." Megan begins to tell what kind of dive she's doing, but she changes her mind. "My dive will be a surprise."

Then I'll keep my dive a surprise, too, you think as you head toward the locker room. You decide it will be a dive you have always wanted to try: a back somersault with one and a half twists.

 Turn to page 59.

"I have a history test to study for—not fun," you tell Riley as you head toward the dorm.

"Good luck," she says in her usual cheery way. But as she walks off toward the lake, you wish you'd told her what's really bothering you. Riley is a great listener and friend.

"Unlike me," you mutter under your breath. You and Megan were best friends before diving—and jealousy—got in the way. What happened?

You meet Megan in her room after dinner. Groaning, Megan opens her textbook. "I'll never, ever remember all these dates and events," she says. She holds out her hand, her fingers spread. "Look at my fingernails. I've been so worried about the test that I chewed them all off."

That surprises you. What also surprises you is how brave Megan is to confess her fear to you. It makes you want to reach out and help her.

"We could make a timeline," you say to Megan. "Timelines help me remember what happened when."

"Great idea," Megan says. "Will you show me how to make one?"

"Glad to," you say, opening your notebook.

 Turn to page 84.

You practice the next day on the trampoline. "You need to find the rhythm of this dive before trying it off the board," Coach tells you.

Rhythm means music, you think. As you walk back to your room after practice, you listen to songs on your MP3 player. You visualize the dive while you run through different songs. Finally, you find one that matches the tempo of the dive: "Let's Fly to the Stars."

The next day, with the song in your head, you again practice on the trampoline. This time you twist gracefully and land on your feet, arms by your sides. "Big difference in that back press!" Coach praises. "Are you ready to try it off the board?"

You nod excitedly and rush to the pool. Luckily, the other girls finished practice half an hour ago, so you won't have an audience.

Confidently, you stride to the end of the board and balance on your toes. You perform a layout back somersault in the air. Toes pointed, legs straight, you twist one and a half times around and then square out, facing away from the board. You slice feetfirst into the water.

When you pop to the surface, you see that Megan is standing next to Coach. Megan smiles and gives you a thumbs-up. Your dive isn't a secret anymore, but that's okay. The mock competition is tomorrow, and everyone will watch as you nail your new dive, just as you did today.

 Turn to page 61.

"I've got the two-and-a-half down pretty well," you boast. You don't want Megan to think that you need help. Your pride is bruised enough.

"Cool," Jamie pipes up from behind you. "Can you show me how to do one?" *Uh-oh.*

"I'd love to see it, too," Emmy chimes in. "Are you going to put it on your dive sheet for the competition?"

The girls look at you, waiting for an answer. At that moment, your stomach starts doing its own somersaults. What are you going to tell your teammates?

If you keep bragging, turn to page 64.

If you realize that bragging will get you into trouble, turn to page 66.

It's the day of the mock competition, and you're pumped. You still don't know what dive Megan is doing, but in the locker room, she hints that it has a higher degree of difficulty than anything she's ever done.

You shrug off Megan's boast, confident that your back twister will be awesome, too.

Pulling your MP3 player from your duffel bag, you sit on the bench and plug in your headphones. You scroll to find the playlist that has "Let's Fly to the Stars," but when you click on the playlist, it's *empty*.

The playlist was full of songs yesterday after practice. You played "Let's Fly to the Stars" for all the girls to hear and told them how it . . .

Wait a minute. You eye your teammates as they take off their warm-ups. You look pointedly at Megan. She's so competitive. Did she erase your song so that she would have an advantage? Or does Jamie want to win so badly that she erased your song as a cruel prank?

If you accuse Megan, turn to page 67.

If you accuse Jamie, turn to page 78.

Playlist empty

Maybe you need to start focusing on fun instead of on being a champion. *That's Megan's dream*, you realize. It might not be the right dream for you.

At the next practice, you bring a boombox into the exercise room. Coach has been having the team work on conditioning. It's important but kind of boring.

With Coach's permission, you pop a CD into the boombox. Soon tunes are filling the room. Jamie dances as she lifts hand weights. Emmy skips to the beat with the jump rope, and you and Megan sing and pretend to hold microphones while you do sit-ups.

The joy the team is feeling spreads to diving practice. You whoop as you sail through the air and plunge into the pool. This is what you love—the exhilaration of spinning, twisting, and flying, as if you were a diving bird.

Later, when Megan comes to your dorm room to tell you she's going to work with a new coach at a clinic, you don't feel jealous at all. You wish her luck. You'd love to be a champion—but you don't want to spend six hours a day practicing and missing out on all the fun.

Before Megan leaves, Isabel pops her head into your room and asks, "Can you guys help out next week with the 'Care and Share' clothing drive?"

"I'm too busy with diving," Megan says.

"But I'd love to!" you pipe up. Isabel's smile lets you know that you made the right decision—for you.

 Turn to page 72.

"I'll definitely put it on my list of dives," you say quickly, before you can chicken out again.

"Me too," Megan says, linking her arm through yours. "Now let's go show the others how it's done."

Grinning with false confidence, you follow Megan up the ladder to the three-meter springboard. *Okay*, you tell yourself. *You've been practicing this. Give it your best try.*

Megan goes first, and the cheers from poolside tell you her dive was good. Now it's your turn. Taking a deep breath, you focus your mind on those somersaults. You walk down the board and hurdle into the air, making only one and a half rotations before kicking out.

When you swim over to the edge, Coach meets you. She squats so that only you can hear her. "Remember, if you put the dive on your sheet and don't complete all the somersaults, you'll get zero points," she warns.

You nod. Tears blur your eyes, but you can't let your teammates see them. When you climb from the water, you're smiling instead.

"You'll get it next time," Emmy says.

"Practice makes perfect," Riley chimes in.

Even Megan has something nice to say: "You'll perfect that dive in no time," she says. "I know you will."

You sigh inside, wishing you had as much confidence in yourself as your teammates have in you.

 Turn to page 71.

Well, yeah, sort of. If you hadn't been so focused on your own problems, you would have noticed that your teammates had feelings and opinions, too.

"How do you handle it?" you ask Riley. "Any advice about controlling my 'Megan envy'?"

Riley giggles. "Megan envy? That's funny," she says. "Actually, humor is a great way to keep things from bothering you. Another way is to try to compete against yourself, not against your teammates."

"Against myself?" you ask, shooting her a puzzled look.

"Yeah. Set mini goals for yourself, like making your *own* dives better each day," she says. "That way you won't be comparing yourself to anyone else."

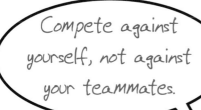
Turn to page 79.

Compete against yourself, not against your teammates.

"I have a confession to make," you say finally. "I've been bragging about a dive that I can't actually do."

Your teammates stare at you. You flush, realizing they have every right to be mad and chew you out.

"That's the big confession?" Emmy finally asks.

Embarrassed, you nod. "I'm sorry, guys. I should have been up-front from the beginning," you say sadly.

Jamie snorts. "If I counted every time I bragged about something I couldn't do," she says, "I'd run out of fingers—and toes."

Emmy giggles. "My big brag was when I said I did that armstand backward somersault off the platform," she says.

"You didn't do it?" Megan asks in surprise.

"Oh, I did it all right," Emmy says, "but I landed smack on my butt."

Everyone laughs.

"Megan, you're the only one who can do the two-and-a-half in the competition," you tell your friend. Admitting it makes you feel lighter. You wish your stubborn pride hadn't kept you from owning up to the truth earlier.

"Actually, I could use more help with the two-and-a-half," Megan confesses. Instantly, the others talk about dives they're having trouble with, too.

"Let's help each other," you suggest. "Together we can master those tricky dives before the competition."

 Turn to page 70.

As your teammates leave the locker room, you catch up with Megan. You hesitate and then ask, "Did you erase my new diving song from my MP3 player?"

Megan stops walking and stares at you. "Why would I erase it?" she asks.

"To win!" you say. "That's all you've been talking about."

Megan looks as if she just took a punch to the stomach. Then she gets mad. "I can't believe you think I'd do something so mean," she snaps. Giving you one last angry look, she stomps off.

Okay, you deserved that scolding. Megan is your friend, yet you wasted no time accusing her. You need to apologize, but it's time for practice—and you desperately need it.

Without being able to warm up with your special song, your timing is off on the back twister. You score threes and fours, while you were hoping for sixes.

"Good try!" Riley says as you climb from the pool.

"It would've been better if I'd warmed up with 'Let's Fly to the Stars,'" you complain. "But it was deleted."

"Oh," Riley says. "Did you erase it by mistake last night?"

"Huh?" you say, thinking back to last night. You and Riley were downloading some music together.

"You didn't have much room on your MP3 player, and you deleted some old songs," says Riley. "Remember?"

You flush with embarrassment. Of course that's what happened—and here you went and accused Megan. Wow.

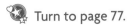 Turn to page 77.

"Thanks, Megan, but I'm following Coach's advice," you tell her. "I need a break."

Megan's face falls. She shrugs and hurries back to the pool. You know you made the right choice—even if it did hurt Megan's feelings. Plus now you'll have time to work on that history project. At least you can make Shelby happy. *But what would make* me *happy?* you wonder.

As you walk down the path toward Starfire Lake, you see Emmy down by the boathouse. She must be waiting for Riley.

"Hey!" Emmy calls when she sees you. "What's up? I thought you'd still be at the pool."

"Coach told me I need a break from diving," you tell her. "I've been practicing so hard all week."

"That's for sure," Emmy agrees. "Maybe you need some time *on* the water instead of *in* the water. Want to come kayaking with Riley, Shelby, and me?"

"Yes!" you say immediately.

When the rest of the girls arrive, you start paddling your kayak toward the other side of the lake. You paddle beside Shelby, who's a beginning kayaker, just like you. When she accidentally bumps into your boat, you turn around and make a silly face at her. She giggles as you both try to straighten back out.

Kayaking with friends is just what I needed, you think.

 Turn to page 76.

You and your teammates pitch in and help one another. By the day of the competition, the whole team is polished, excited, and ready to go! As expected, Megan shines, taking first place on the team *and* in the overall competition. That's an incredible accomplishment, and you are proud of your friend.

You aren't even number two—Emmy has that honor. But the Innerstar U team wins the competition! It's the first "first" for the team, and you and your teammates jump and cheer wildly.

When it's time for the photo to be taken for the school newspaper, Megan hands you the team trophy. "You should hold this," she says. "You were the one who kept encouraging us to work together."

You beam as you hold that trophy high for the team picture. You weren't number one on the team or in the competition, but being number three on a *team* that was number one makes you feel just as proud.

The End

The next day, when you fill out your dive sheet, you quickly jot down "104C"—the dive number for the forward two-and-a-half tuck. You have another day to practice it, and you're almost there, right?

You head back to the three-meter springboard. After three more tries, you finally hold on for the full two and a half rotations, but it's not pretty.

"Your tuck is too loose," Coach tells you. "Try grabbing your shins closer to your ankles."

On your last try, you hold your shins in a tighter tuck. You spin faster, but your eyes are closed, so you miss your spot and go over. Coach points out that you need to keep your eyes open.

One more thing I'm doing wrong, you think tiredly.

But when competition day arrives, you stubbornly keep dive number 104C on your list. You're determined to go for that two-and-a-half.

 Turn to page 73.

Isabel and you "dive" into the clothing drive. First you make colorful posters to hang up on the dorm walls. Then you put huge collection boxes in each hallway. Last, you start going through your own closet.

You're trying to decide if you should toss that awful flowered blouse your aunt gave you when Megan comes into the room. Her head hangs and she's dragging her feet.

"What's wrong?" you ask worriedly.

Megan throws herself onto your desk chair, looking totally dejected. "The coach at the clinic says I'm not ready to train with her yet," she says. "The other girls in her clinic have been diving for years." Megan sighs.

You know how focused your friend is on becoming a champion. This must feel like the end of the world to her. How can you help her get through it?

"I bet wearing this gorgeous flowered blouse will perk you up," you tease.

Megan can't help laughing.

"Hey, why don't you join Isabel and me with the clothing drive?" you ask. "We sure could use the help."

"I can see that," says Megan. Plucking the blouse from your grasp, she throws it into the clothes box. "Okay. Count me in."

 Turn to page 74.

You huddle on the bench, worrying about the dive, until Emmy calls your name. "You're up!" she tells you.

Blowing out a breath, you leave the bench and walk toward the springboard. *Focus,* you tell yourself.

You wait for your dive to be announced. Then you step forward. You handle the approach confidently, leap into the air, and grab your shins as you somersault. Halfway through your dive, though, your mind flashes back to the announcement you just heard: "Forward two somersaults tuck." *Two somersaults?* What happened to the two-and-a-half? Did you write down the wrong dive number?

In your confusion, you botch the dive. You hit the water awkwardly and quickly pop to the surface, gasping. It takes only a minute for the judges to give you five zeros. You *did* write down the wrong number. You should have written "105C." Your teammates look stunned.

Silently, you dry off with your chamois. You don't even want to look at the others on the bench.

Megan is the last diver to go on the Innerstar U team. She saved the two-and-a-half somersault for last. It's not perfect—she scores fives—but you would have *loved* fives!

Next time you'll spend less time bragging and worrying about what Megan's doing. You'll take more time prepping for the competition—and filling out your dive sheet. You'll practice a dive you've chosen until you truly are confident. That's the *only* way to shine.

The End

Jumping up, Megan channels her energy into sorting your closet. "You won't wear these again, will you?" she asks, holding up an outfit with a whole lot of ruffles. Before you can answer, she wads up the clothes and shoots them like a basketball into the donation box. Soon you're both giggling, and the box is full.

"Just wait until I sort through *your* closet," you tease as you drag the overflowing box into the hall.

When you go through Megan's closet, you find shoes and uniforms for every sport. "You sure do like sports," you say.

"I do," Megan agrees as she drops old soccer cleats into the box. "And one day, I *will* make the national team."

"I believe you," you say sincerely. Until Megan joined the dive team, you never knew how competitive she was. *But competitive can be good,* you think as you lug the boxes Megan helped you collect down to the dorm lobby.

You, Megan, and Isabel count the boxes in the lobby: twenty-two! "That has to be a record for the clothing drive," Isabel says. She reaches into her pocket and pulls out two gold star pins. "Innerstar U says thank you!" she says, handing you and Megan each a pin.

Grinning, Megan says, "I guess there's more than one way to bring home the gold."

"And to be a champion," you add as you proudly pin a star onto your good friend's shirt.

The End

After kayaking, you and Shelby head to the dorm to finish that history project. She holds up the poster, which is covered with stunning photos of Greece. Shelby added captions beneath each one.

"Wow, you did a great job," you tell her.

"Thanks. I left space for you," she says, tapping a blank spot on the poster.

You flush. "Er, sorry I wasn't a better partner," you say.

"No worries," says Shelby. "Emmy told me how hard you've been practicing."

"Still, schoolwork and friendship should come first," you insist. "I wasn't being a good friend by making you do all the work."

You listen to yourself, amazed at the words coming out of your mouth. If you truly believed that friendship comes first, wouldn't you be a better friend to Megan?

You try to push Megan from your mind and put all your energy into finishing up the history project. You help Shelby fill the blank space and add a pretty border to the poster. When it's done, Shelby holds it up.

"This is A-plus work," she says, and you agree. Working together was fun. You only wish you'd helped Shelby more from the start.

 Turn to page 90.

Head down, you walk to the bench. You make it through the rest of your dives, but your heart's not in them.

Megan is the last to dive. With her back straight and her head held high, she approaches, springs into the air, and performs a terrific front two-and-a-half tuck on the one-meter. You clap as loudly as your teammates. Fortunately, your accusation didn't keep Megan from doing her best. The judges of the mock competition give her the sixes you wanted—but didn't earn.

You hurry over to greet Megan as she climbs from the pool. As you hand Megan her chamois, you quickly say, "Terrific dive. I would have given you a ten."

Megan looks sideways at you. Silently she dries off, as if waiting for you to say something more.

"I'm so sorry, Megan," you blurt. "I never should have accused you of erasing my music."

Megan nods. "Apology accepted," she says quietly. "I know you were stressed over that dive."

Before you can say more, Coach calls all of you back to the bench. "Gather round, team," she says. "Let's talk about what this mock competition taught each of us."

You already know what your answer is going to be. You learned to think first before accusing anyone—and to never be too proud to admit your mistakes.

The End

Jamie is the last to leave the locker room. "Did you erase a song from my MP3 player?" you ask her.

"Don't tell me that someone erased the song you've been blabbing about for two days," she says. "What a great prank. I wish I *had* thought of it."

"Why would you—or someone else—do something so mean?" you ask angrily.

Jamie pulls her chamois from her athletic bag. "For one," she says, "you've been so focused on your own dives that you forgot about the rest of us. But whatever. I didn't do it, so go accuse someone else." She marches from the locker room, leaving you alone.

You hear the excited chatter of your teammates echoing throughout the pool area. The mock competition must have started, which means you don't have time to dwell on this any longer.

When it's time to perform your back somersault one-and-a-half twist, you try humming "Let's Fly to the Stars." You balance at the end of the board and raise your arms. Springing backward, you somersault and twist. But you're so flustered by everything that has happened, you forget that extra half twist.

Dejected, you climb from the pool. You don't need to look at your scores. Forgetting that half twist means you failed the dive. Zeroes for you.

 Turn to page 83.

That's great advice, you think. Maybe it's time to start competing against *yourself* instead of against Megan and everyone else.

At the next practice, you feel much more enthusiastic. Coach helps you work on the two-and-a-half in belts on the trampoline while Riley shouts encouragement from the side. This time you don't think about Megan and how fast she mastered the trick. This time you listen to Coach and to Riley, and you focus on your own ability to master the skill.

By the end of the hour, you are gracefully kicking out straight up and down.

"Whew!" you exclaim. "Finally!"

Riley laughs. "Feels good, huh?" she says. Then she tilts her head and asks, "Ready to try it off the board?"

Immediately, your stomach tightens. You take a deep breath and push through it. "Ready," you say.

All your hard work pays off. You rotate in the air and slice into the water without a hitch.

"Woo-hoo!" Riley cheers when you surface.

"*You're* the one who deserves a cheer," you tell her. "You and I may not be the number-one divers on the team, but you're a number-one friend and coach."

Thanks to Riley, you learned that competing against yourself is a great way to train. But when it comes to celebrating your success, you're glad to have your team-mates by your side.

The End

A few days later, you borrow a leotard from Neely and join her at ballet class. Neely shows you some stretches. She has you sit on the floor and straighten your legs out in front of you.

"Stretch your toes back toward you," she says. "These are called 'Aladdin toes' because they make your feet look like a genie's slippers, don't they? Now stretch your toes back down toward the floor."

Staring at your outstretched toes, it occurs to you that this stretch might help with diving. "When we leave the board, we have to keep our toes pointed just like this," you say to Neely.

She smiles as she helps you up. "Do the stretch every day, then," she says, "and pretty soon you'll have perfect toe-points!"

Next she shows you basic arm movements, called *port de bras.* As you move your arms through the positions, Neely reminds you to keep your chin up and your shoulders down. You do exactly the opposite: raise your shoulders and lower your chin. Oops! "I had no idea ballet was so complicated," you say, giggling.

Afterward, though, you feel more graceful. Coach is always mentioning that you need to dive as gracefully as a dancer. Now you *are* one! Well, not yet, but this is fun, and you tell Neely that you can't wait to come back.

 Turn to page 82.

You enjoy ballet and gymnastics so much that you start doing both once a week. It does make the week hectic, though, especially with your teammates pushing to learn the harder optional dives for the competition. When Coach starts adding extra diving practices during the week, you know that you're going to have to give up either ballet or gymnastics. But which one?

Ballet improves your posture, and Neely is an awesome teacher. But gymnastics helps you with balance and with your somersaults and twists. You love Isabel and the girls in the club, too.

Neither ballet nor gymnastics has helped you deal with Megan, you realize. Actually, you really haven't seen her that much since you started the other activities.

Your head swims as you think about your choices. What are you going to do?

 If you decide to stick with gymnastics, turn to page 86.

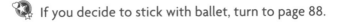 If you decide to stick with ballet, turn to page 88.

Riley comes over and says, "Good try. You'll get it next time."

"Yeah, sure," you grumble. Stomping into the locker room, you plop onto the bench.

Jamie's right. In your mission to outdo Megan, you have ignored your teammates. You went about winning the wrong way—focusing only on yourself. That's just part of being a good athlete. The other part is being a good teammate. Right now, you're neither. You blew your dive as a competitor, and you blew being a good teammate when you accused Jamie.

Riley pokes her head through the locker-room doorway. "Are you okay?" she asks hesitantly.

You feel a sudden rush of guilt. "Sorry I was such a grump," you say to Riley. "I was just bummed about the dive. This mock competition showed me that I don't have what it takes to be a good diver, and now I'm being a rotten teammate, too." You slump forward, your chin in your hands.

 If you ask Riley for help, turn to page 87.

 If you decide to quit the dive team, turn to page 89.

As you and Megan work, she says, "You know, I may be a daredevil in sports. But when it comes to a history test, I'm a big chicken."

You glance up at Megan's anxious face. Maybe now would be a good time to confess your diving fears to her. "You know," you say, "the reason I quit practice early today was because I couldn't get that two-and-a-half. I got scared that I was going to blow it."

Megan nods. "Like me and this test," she says. "I don't want to get an F."

"You *won't*," you tell her firmly. "I'll help you."

"And you'll get a great score on that two-and-a-half," she tells you, just as sincerely. "I'll make sure."

Megan keeps her word. The next day during practice, you work in belts on the trampoline. Coach spots you, and Megan and your other teammates crowd around, offering suggestions. With their help, you do a pretty decent two-and-a-half.

Then you ask, "Who's next? You guys all helped me master that trick. Now it's my turn to help you."

 Turn to page 94.

It's a tough choice, but gymnastics wins. At the next practice, Isabel tells you that the club is performing at a school assembly on Saturday morning. "Do you want to do a routine with me?" she asks.

"Absolutely!" you say. But then it hits you—the diving competition is on the *same* day. The truth is, you'd much rather do gymnastics. You love to learn new skills without the pressure of competing. You decide to talk with your dive teammates and find out if they really need you on Saturday.

"No problem," Jamie says bluntly when you tell your teammates your dilemma. "Megan has kind of taken over your number-two spot anyway."

So much for being worried about their reactions, you think.

Then Riley puts her arm around you. "But you'll still practice with us, right?" she asks sweetly.

"Of course," you say. "I love diving. I just don't love competing."

"That's funny," says Megan, "because competing is the part I really *like*." She gives you a big smile. "Thanks for introducing me to diving, BFF."

"Thanks for introducing me to gymnastics, BFF," you say, grinning back at her. The two of you bump fists. This is the closest you've felt to Megan in a long time. The solution to your friendship problems just took a little creativity!

 Turn to page 96.

You want to crawl into a hole, but it doesn't look as if Riley is going anywhere, so you decide to let her in and ask her for help. "Riley," you finally say, "I wish I knew how to be a better teammate. Any words of wisdom?"

Riley sits next to you. "Well," she begins, "I try to focus on a goal besides winning. Then I don't get so flustered before a dive—or so disappointed when I get low scores."

That sounds like a great idea. "What's your goal?" you ask Riley.

"I try to learn new dives for the team," she explains. "And I work hard to be a good sport instead of a sore loser."

A sore loser? That sounds like someone you know. *Face it*, you think, *messing up the dive was your own fault.* If you had practiced more, you could have performed the dive even if you hadn't warmed up with the song.

 Turn to page 95.

Try to focus on a goal besides winning.

"I'm so happy you decided to join ballet!" Neely exclaims when you tell her your decision. She helps you pick out a leotard—berry-colored like your swimsuit.

Ballet really helps you relax. The positions are slow and graceful, and Neely shows you how to breathe deeply. And, wow, those toe-point exercises really do the trick. Even Coach praises you during diving practice. "Nice feet!" she says. "Remember that your feet are the last thing the judges see. If they're perfect, it leaves the judges with a good impression—and you with a better score."

"That was a great compliment Coach gave you," Emmy says as the two of you head back toward the boards. "You do have nice form. What's your secret?"

Your eyes twinkle as you confess your big "secret." "It's ballet," you tell Emmy.

She nods. "That makes sense. Coach is always saying how ballet can help our diving. I just wish I had time to fit another activity into my schedule," she says.

That gives you an idea. "Maybe you won't *have* to," you say to Emmy.

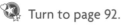 Turn to page 92.

"Diving isn't fun anymore," you tell Riley. "If I can't be a good diver or a good teammate, I should just quit."

"What?" Riley says, eyes wide. "That's drastic. Don't you think you should talk to the rest of the team first?"

You blow out your breath. You doubt that the rest of the team will miss you after the way you've acted. "I don't think they'll give me any reason *not* to quit," you say.

"Quit?" asks Emmy as she walks into the locker room. Jamie and Megan are right behind her.

"You can't quit!" Jamie and Megan pipe up.

"Why not?" you mumble, staring at your feet.

"I can think of a *lot* of reasons why not," Emmy says. She counts off on her fingers: "One, you always have new ideas to make practice fun. Two, you bring music to share during exercise."

"Three, you're fun to play pranks on," adds Jamie, grinning.

"Four, you do the best front twister on the whole team," Riley says.

"And five, you're our friend," Megan says solemnly.

Wow, you had no idea they felt that way. "Thanks, guys," you say, your voice thick with tears. "I needed that."

Your teammates sure came through for you, and that helps you make your decision. You'll stick with the team. But from now on, you promise yourself, you're going to focus on *team* pride instead of on "me" pride.

The End

A day at the lake and time with Shelby make you feel like a new girl—until diving practice the next day. When you say hi to Megan in the locker room, she gives you a hurt look. What's that all about?

"I heard a bunch of you went to the lake yesterday," she says bluntly. "Thanks for inviting *me*." Grabbing her towel, she heads out to the pool.

Uh-oh. You've managed to hurt Megan's feelings again. You should probably apologize, but what can you say— "I just needed a break from you, Megan"? That would be really hurtful.

Stomach twisting, you join your teammates by the side of the pool. Coach is talking about the interscholastic competition. "There will be six schools competing," she says, "including Hillside, who beat us last year."

"They won't beat us *this* year," Jamie declares. "We've worked too hard."

"And now we have Megan on our team," Emmy adds.

You don't even want to think about the competition. You know that Megan will outshine you. And now that she's mad at you, you feel not only like a lousy diver but like a lousy friend, too.

If you hold your head high and decide to do your best, turn to page 93.

If you decide to drown your sorrows in ice cream, turn to page 106.

Competition Prep

☑ Diving sheets

☑ Schedule

☑ Team/individual goals

☐

☐

☐

You decide to show your teammates what you've learned in ballet. At the beginning of the next practice, you teach them the toe-flexing exercise that Neely taught you. "Stretch your toes and ankles forward, making a long, beautiful line. Hold it as long as you can, and then relax," you explain.

"Wow," Emmy says as she points and flexes her feet. "I can see how this exercise will really help."

Emmy's right. By the day of the competition, everyone's form is better. Megan gets a seven on a back somersault one-half twist. Riley earns an average score of seven for an inward dive. And *you* earn a score of seven with a reverse dive.

Emmy is the last to go. You hold your breath as she does a reverse one-and-a-half-somersault tuck. You think she nailed it. Will the judges agree?

The judges hold up their scores: *all* sevens! The team explodes with excitement.

Emmy looks shocked. "I can't believe we all earned sevens!" she says, grinning from ear to ear.

"Nothing's impossible when you work hard," Riley says as she puts her arm around Emmy.

"And when you and your friends have fun working *together*," Megan adds, looking straight at you!

The End

You remember what Megan said about focusing on what you do right instead of on what you do wrong. The problem is, you haven't been doing too many things right lately. If you're going to improve in time for the next competition, you need to seriously fix some things.

"In a few days, I'll need the lists of dives you'll be doing in the competition," Coach says.

Most of your teammates head off in a group toward the boards, talking about their dives. You walk in the opposite direction to warm up with laps in the pool. A warm-up will help you stretch your muscles *and* your brain.

As you swim down the lap lane, you think about what you need to improve on. Team spirit, that's for sure. You've been so focused on yourself that you hurt Megan's feelings. But if you're going to do well at the competition, you also need to work on harder dives, starting with that two-and-a-half.

 If you decide to work on team spirit, turn to page 97.

 If you decide to work on dives, turn to page 117.

"I'm ready," Riley says, stepping up for a turn on the trampoline. "I've always wanted to try the back one-and-a-half, but I'm afraid I'll land on my back."

"I was afraid of the two-and-a-half, too," you tell her as she buckles her harness. "But with Megan's and everyone's help, I managed to work through being scared."

Riley gives you a grateful smile. "Then I can do it, too," she says confidently.

You and your teammates circle around the trampoline.

"You can do it, Ri!" Emmy shouts.

Jamie whoops, and Megan and Coach call out a few suggestions.

As you holler encouragement to Riley, you think that next time, you won't keep your fear inside. You won't stew about it until it makes you half crazy. Admitting your fear not only helped you, but it helped everyone else, too. In fact, practice the rest of the week goes really well. The team is heading into the weekend competition with a few new dives and newfound bravery.

Best of all, the Friday afternoon before the competition, Megan runs into your dorm room waving a paper. "Look!" she calls to you proudly. "I got my first A on a history test—thanks to my best friend!"

The End

"I like the way you think, Riley," you tell your friend. "I definitely need to work on being a better sport. But the first thing I should do is apologize to Jamie."

You and Riley head back to the pool area. The mock competition is almost over. Jamie performs her last dive, a front dive one-half twist. It doesn't have a high degree of difficulty, but she does it well and scores sixes and sevens.

"Wow! Great dive, Jamie," you tell her as she dries off. "And I'm really, really sorry I accused you of erasing that song," you add.

Jamie shrugs. "I can see why you blamed me," she says. "I mean, it *does* sound like something I would do." She gives you a sly smile.

You're glad Jamie isn't mad. Next step: You'll follow Riley's advice and find some new dives to master with your teammates. It'll be fun to work *with* them instead of always trying to outdo them.

"Why don't you try platform diving with me?" Emmy suggests when you tell her your new goal.

"I've always wanted to learn synchronized diving," Megan says. "We could do it together."

Wow, you love both ideas. Which should you choose?

If you like the idea of synchronized diving, turn to page 98.

If you like the idea of platform diving, turn to page 102.

You and Isabel choose music for your gymnastics routine and get to work on your choreography. She teaches you front and back walkovers, which you've never done before. Your balance and strength from diving help you learn the new moves quickly.

Saturday, your routine is a success! The audience gives you and Isabel a standing ovation. Best of all, your diving teammates are in the front row, wearing their berry-colored team warm-ups. They have to leave halfway through the assembly to head to the diving competition, but you're glad they saw your routine. As soon as you're done, you hurry to the pool, too. You want to be in the audience there, cheering for your friends.

The sports center is crowded with divers from different teams. A teeny part of you wishes you were suited up, too, until Isabel plunks down next to you in the bleachers. She's carrying pom-poms in Innerstar U team colors so that the two of you can cheer for your team.

Megan is the first diver for Innerstar U. You hold your breath as she climbs onto the three-meter springboard. For a second, she seems frozen. Then she strides forward, springs into the air, and twirls in a two-and-a-half before plunging headfirst into the water.

The judges award her eights. Wow! Your diving teammates burst into cheers. Jumping to your feet, *you* clap for your friend the loudest of all.

The End

Diving is an individual sport *and* a team sport. You want to do well on your own, sure, but you also need to be there for your team. That means rooting for everyone—even Megan. But how can you set aside your jealousy?

You know the person to ask—the best cheerleader at school: Riley. When you finish your laps, you catch up to Riley, who's just coming out of the pool from a dive.

"I need some cheerleading tips," you tell her as she dries off with her chamois. "Ways to cheer on our team."

Riley raises her brows. "That sounds like fun," she says. Then she launches into a long list of ideas. Obviously, she was the right girl to ask.

When she's finished, you exclaim, "Thanks, Riley! You helped me come up with a great idea. I can't wait to share it with the team."

If you invite the team to watch a diving DVD, turn to page 104.

If you invite the team to decorate team T-shirts, turn to page 112.

You and Megan watch Emmy and Riley practice a synchronized dive. The two perform exactly the same dive off boards that are side by side.

"Fun!" Megan says. "I'm glad we decided to try this."

"Fun—but hard, too," you point out. "Emmy and Riley had to get their timing just right."

"Piece of cake," Megan says.

The next day, you try synchronizing your approaches, but Megan strides down the board either too slow or too fast. Next, you both try a back dive. This time, *you* always leave too early or too late.

"This is frustrating," you tell Megan on your tenth try.

She nods. "And boring. When do we get to try some harder dives?"

"First we have to learn how to do the approach and hurdle at the same time," you explain.

Megan sighs. "I think I've had enough for one day," she says. "I need to practice my back somersaults." She waves and heads down the diving board without you.

So much for being in sync, you think.

Turn to page 101.

You've always wanted to do an inward dive straight in a competition. It's not a difficult dive, but you have only a week before the competition, so you need to choose a dive that you're confident you can master.

You remember Neely's words about shining in her small role—and supporting the other actors, too. If you shine at this dive, you'll earn good points, which will support your whole team.

The day of the competition, you stride confidently to the end of the board and turn around so that your back faces the pool. Balancing on your toes, you raise your arms. When you are steady and poised, you jump strong and swing your arms high over your head. Snapping your heels back behind you, you set to a perfect T with your arms and body, rotating forward as straight as an arrow until you're lined up and entering the pool headfirst.

When you swim to the surface, you feel like a star in the spotlight. Your teammates are cheering for you, and you earn a score of seven, which boosts your team into first place. Yay!

You're proud that you were able to get over your hurt feelings and concentrate on diving. When your team poses for photos after the competition, everyone is shining brightly—but no one quite as brightly as you!

The End

Your second practice doesn't go any better. Megan wants to rush ahead and do harder dives before your timing is even close to being synced up.

"We have to concentrate on getting our timing right on easier dives," you tell Megan. You know you sound huffy, but you've been working on a front dive for an hour and it isn't going well.

"How can I concentrate when this is so boring?" Megan grumbles. "We do the same thing over and over and . . ."

You cross your arms. "If you'd quit pushing to do harder dives, we might get our timing right," you say pointedly.

"If you wouldn't be so bossy about the basics, I might quit pushing," she snaps back. "I don't even want to do this anymore." She whirls around and marches off to the locker room.

You almost call out after her, but you stop yourself. Maybe synchronized diving wasn't the right choice. It's certainly not making you a better teammate, and it's taking a toll on your already strained friendship.

 Turn to page 105.

Platform diving might be the perfect solution. Megan doesn't do platform, so you won't keep comparing yourself to your friend. Plus, platform diving will put your focus in the right place—on learning a new skill.

You talk it over with Coach, who tells you that it's a challenge you're ready for. "Your entries are tight, which is important in platform diving," Coach explains.

In the exercise room, Emmy gives you more pointers. "In platform takeoffs, strong jumps are important," she says. "You need to really exercise your leg muscles." She shows you how to practice your takeoffs on the mat until you get the motion down.

Back at the pool, Emmy and Coach start you on the five-meter—which still seems really high, you think, as you watch Emmy climb the stairs to the top. She shows you a simple dive from the platform and then motions for you to take a turn.

You climb the steps carefully and step out onto the platform. You're surprised to find that it's solid concrete. You're so used to a flexible board that the platform feels strange under your feet.

Gulping, you walk to the end of the platform and look down. It's only two meters higher than a springboard. Who knew it would look so *scary*?

 Turn to page 109.

Watching a diving movie seems like the best way to get the team together, and your teammates love the idea.

"Let's do it Thursday night," Jamie suggests.

"Perfect!" Emmy agrees.

At the end of practice, you invite Megan to help you buy snacks for movie night. It won't totally make up for not inviting her to the lake, but maybe it will help.

As you and Megan walk to the student center, the two of you start talking about your favorite movies. Soon you remember why you've been such good friends. You enjoy lots of the same things, including the same snacks.

"We definitely need marshmallows, chocolate bars, and graham crackers," Megan says.

"That's right!" you say. "S'mores used to be your favorite."

"They still are," says Megan, grinning. That's when you realize that Megan is the same person you used to have fun with. She didn't change. *You* did. For some reason, when she joined the team, you started treating her like an opponent instead of a friend.

You need to get your friendship back on track. Picking out snacks and having fun together on movie night will be a good start.

 Turn to page 108.

You sulk on the bench for a while. You're frustrated with Megan, but you're a little mad at yourself, too. You *were* being kind of bossy. There has to be a way to fix this, but you may have to make the first move.

Heading into the locker room, you find Megan combing her wet hair. You quickly apologize. "I want you to be my partner," you tell your friend. "I want us to do well in the competition, too. But there must be a better way than me getting on your case all the time."

"I agree totally," Megan says. "Practice was getting to be no fun."

You think for a minute, wondering what you can do to make it better. "I have a suggestion," you say. "Maybe we could practice the basics for half an hour, and then practice a tricky dive for the other half."

"Ooh, I like that idea," Megan says, smiling. "Should we start again tomorrow?"

The two of you leave the sports center arm in arm. You're proud that you came up with a solution. Your synchronized dives may never be great, but if you keep working on it, you bet that your friendship will be.

The End

After practice you make a beeline to the bakery at the student center. "A double vanilla shake," you order. A sweet, creamy drink will definitely drown your sorrows.

Then you spot your friend Neely sitting at one of the round tables. She's huddled over a shake that looks just as big as yours.

When you get your drink, you walk over. "Hey, Neely. Want some company?" you ask. When you see her tear-stained face, you quickly add, "Or not."

"I'd love company," she says, wiping her face and nodding toward the other chair. She forces a smile.

Silently, the two of you sip your shakes. Finally Neely says, "So I didn't get the lead in the school's new musical. I mean, I got a supporting role, but the lead is special." Neely shrugs. "I guess it's just not my turn to shine."

"I know how that feels," you grumble. "My friend Megan is an amazing diver. I can't help feeling jealous."

Neely nods sympathetically. "At first I was jealous of the girl who got the lead," she says, taking another sip. "But I'm starting to get over it."

"How?" you ask. If Neely knows a magic trick for beating jealousy, you'd sure like to hear about it.

 Turn to page 110.

Thursday night, the girls meet in your room. You scatter pillows, a sleeping bag, and a beanbag chair on the floor. Megan pops in the DVD, and you bring out the snacks.

"Who wants a somersault s'more?" you ask. "Or a popcorn cannonball?"

"Or how about a pretzel twist?" Megan chimes in. You've given the snacks silly names, which make the rest of your teammates giggle. But when the DVD starts, the room goes silent. The divers are incredible!

After the movie, your friends start talking about how much harder they're going to work and about adding new dives to their lists. As you settle back, munching on a pretzel twist, you think about how movie night has inspired *you*. From now on, you won't let competing and winning get in the way of friendship.

That decision lets you know that you're ready for this weekend's competition. You'll tackle the dives on your list and perform them as well as you can, but you'll also be there to cheer on Megan and the rest of your teammates. You've found a way to be proud of yourself *and* proud of your team.

The End

Fortunately, Emmy is right behind you. "Just practice the standing forward takeoff," she urges. "And do a feet-first entry."

You breathe a sigh of relief. That sounds easy. But when you spring and jump out, your body tilts backward, and you smack your legs on the water. *Ouch.* You've smacked your legs plenty of times, but it stings worse off the high platform.

Emmy waves at you to come up and try again. You're not a quitter, so you hurry up the stairs. "Are you okay?" she asks, noticing that the backs of your legs are bright red.

Nodding, you try it again. Your fear messes with your focus, though, and you land in the water awkwardly a second time.

Megan is standing at the pool's edge when you surface. As soon as you see your friend, you feel hot tears rush to your eyes. You suddenly wish you had taken her up on synchronized diving. Surely it's easier than this.

If you quit platform and try synchronized diving instead, turn to page 98.

If you stick with platform diving, go online to www.innerstarU.com and enter this code: PROUD2BME

"I had a talk with myself," Neely says. "I told myself, 'Neely, you can shine in whatever role you were given—no matter how small. And you can try to support the other actors, too.'" Neely blushes. "Maybe that sounds silly," she adds.

"No!" you say. "It's great advice, actually. It might work for me, too." Neely has given you two good ideas. You can work harder to support Megan in her role as number-one diver, or you can work hard on your own dives so that you'll shine, too.

If you focus on supporting Megan, turn to page 114.

If you focus on your own diving, turn to page 100.

You can shine in whatever role you were given—no matter how small.

The next time you dive at the pool, you think about Emmy's advice. Shelby records you again as you spin in the air twice and drop cleanly into the water.

"You did it!" shouts Emmy.

"And I've got it all on video!" Shelby calls.

When you swim to the side of the pool, you thank your friends. You don't have to watch yourself on the video recorder to know that your dive was "picture perfect"!

As you get out of the water and head back to the board, you spot Megan walking in from the locker room. She catches your eye and turns away quickly. You feel a twinge of guilt. Now that you've gotten this dive down, it's time to start working on your other goals—and your friendship with Megan tops the list.

The End

The girls love your idea of decorating team T-shirts. You could wear them over your suits at the interscholastic competition—or even around campus to let everyone know about the dive team!

After practice, all the girls walk to Sparkle Studios. Neely and Shelby are there, working on a class project. They help you find the materials you need—including fabric markers in all the colors of the rainbow.

You and your teammates use the markers to write fun messages on your shirts. Emmy writes, "Innerstar U divers have the best team spirit!" Another teammate writes, "Dive Like Dolphins!"

Megan is working silently at the art table. You wonder what she's going to write—something about being number one, you guess. You decide to write something that will remind you to be a better friend to your teammates.

 Turn to page 115.

The interscholastic competition is a week away. Megan has the best chance of earning top points, so you throw yourself into helping your friend perfect the dives on her list.

But on Wednesday after practice, Emmy and Riley pull you aside. "You've barely practiced your own dives lately," Emmy says.

"I've been helping Megan," you tell them.

"But the competition is only two days away," Riley says. "Will *you* be ready? We need your strong dives to help us win."

When they leave, you blow out a frustrated breath. You've been trying to be a good teammate to Megan, but the competition is coming up awfully quickly, and it's true that you haven't been practicing your own dives. What should you do?

 If you start working on your own dives, turn to page 116.

 If you continue to help Megan, turn to page 118.

You hold up your T-shirt at the same time Megan holds up hers. The two of you start laughing, because you've written almost the same thing. Yours says, "Friends + Teammates = Winners!" Hers says, "Divers, Teammates, Friends, Winners!"

You grin at Megan, and she grins back. You wonder if she has been feeling as gloomy as you have since your friendship took a dive. If so, this would be a good time to say something.

As you walk back to the dorm, you apologize to Megan. "I'm sorry," you blurt. "I almost let the competition ruin a great friendship."

"I did, too!" says Megan, who seems relieved that you two are finally talking about this. "Let's promise that from here on out, we'll put our friendship first," she says.

Nodding, you agree.

The team T-shirts are your good-luck charms at the competition. Innerstar U takes first place!

It's not just the T-shirts, you know. It's your team spirit. All day long, you cheer for one another. And when Megan takes first place in the *entire* competition, you cheer loudest for your friend—which makes *you* feel like a winner, too.

The End

Riley and Emmy are right. You need to start practicing the back one-and-a-half somersault one-half twist, which is a new dive for you.

Megan comes over. She's dripping wet and flushed from working so hard. "What's up?" she asks. "Are we done practicing?"

"No. I mean, yes," you say. "Emmy and Riley just reminded me that I need to work on my own dives, too."

You're afraid that Megan will be disappointed, but instead she says, "Great! You've spent so much time helping me. It's time I returned the favor."

Megan hasn't been diving as long as you have, but her gymnastics training has given her a great eye for somersaults and twists. As you practice the dive, she gives you some terrific pointers. With her coaching and a few more tries, you feel as if you have it down.

By the weekend, you're both ready. The judges' scores prove that helping each other worked. Megan and you score sixes and sevens on every dive. You are tied for third place in the rankings and tied for first place on the team. Best of all, your scores push the Innerstar U team to number one!

As the team accepts the trophy, you're bursting with double pride. You are proud of yourself and *just* as proud of your good friend.

The End

You decide to work on dives first. After you master that two-and-a-half, you'll work on being a better teammate.

note to self:
1. Master the two and a half

2. Be a better teammate

Later in the dorm, Shelby gives you a great idea. "Say Swiss cheese!" she says as you're walking down the hall. Shelby's holding a small video recorder.

You give her a cheesy smile and ask, "What's that for?"

"I'm doing a project on campus life," Shelby explains. "Want me to play some of it back for you?"

Your brows rise. That's it! You'll get Shelby to record your two-and-a-half and then play it back so that you can see what you're doing wrong.

At the next practice, Shelby records you. Then you have Emmy watch the video with you. Since she's the best diver on the team, she'll be able to pick out your mistakes.

"When you start the somersault, your arms are going to the sides instead of straight down," Emmy points out. "That's why it's hard making it all the way around."

Aha! That makes perfect sense. You're feeling a lot more hopeful now about mastering the dive.

 Turn to page 111.

You understand why Emmy and Riley are worried, but when you check over your list of dives, you decide they're easy enough that you won't have to practice too much. You'd rather help Megan. Being a good friend to her keeps your jealousy in check.

As you watch the other schools' divers on the day of the competition, though, you realize that Emmy and Riley weren't exaggerating. The competition is *tough*. The simple dives you put on your sheet aren't going to cut it!

Toward the end of the meet, you're feeling heavy with disappointment. Your low degrees of difficulty have hurt your overall total. On the bright side, every time Megan scores sixes and sevens, you feel little bursts of pride.

At the end of the competition, Megan wraps her arms around you in a huge hug.

"You were awesome!" you tell her, and it's the truth.

"Only because I had an awesome coach," Megan insists.

You beam. You enjoyed "coaching" Megan almost as much as you enjoy diving yourself. Maybe one day, you'll talk to Coach about being an assistant.

For the next competition, you'll balance your time better. But today, you're proud to be called "coach"—and proud to call your friend "winner."

The End